Always M

By Mandy Al-Bjaly

My dear daughter, I have always thought of you as my Princess, but you are more grown up now, and don't dress up like a princess much anymore.

You probably feel that you are getting a little too old for fairy-tale princess stories too, but let me help you see these stories in another way. I want you to see why you are, and will always be, my Princess.

As you know, in the very best fairy tales, the princesses are beautiful inside and out. They have qualities we all wish to have and do good deeds we all wish to mirror. ***There are so many lessons I want you to learn from the classic fairy-tale princess stories.***

Briar Rose, who we usually call Sleeping Beauty, received generous gifts at birth from seven good fairies. The first six were beauty, wit, grace, dance, song, and kindness. The final gift saved her from an evil fairy's curse of death by a spinning wheel. I want you to use your special gifts and talents to bless others.

James 1:17

"The Good Fairy's Promise" by Léon Bakst

Cinderella was humble and tender-hearted. Her life was very hard, but she didn't complain. She spent her days obediently serving her cruel stepmother and stepsisters and spent her nights sleeping by the fireplace. She forgave them for how cruelly they treated her. I want you to try your best to love your enemies and do good to them.

Matthew 5:44, Ephesians 4:32

"Stepsisters" from Journeys through Bookland

Beauty loved her father more than her own life and possessions. She willingly surrendered herself to a beast in exchange for her father's freedom. Though it was hard to be apart from her family, she was kind to the Beast and saw goodness in him, even learning to love him. I want you to never judge others by the way they look, but instead to love and respect them for their minds and hearts.

1 Samuel 16:7

"Beauty and the Beast" by Walter Crane

Rapunzel had an angelic singing voice and golden hair that reached down a tower where a witch kept her locked away. Through her song, she and a prince found each other, fell in love, and secretly married. The jealous witch cut Rapunzel's hair and banished her. Her heartbroken prince threw himself from the tower where thorns blinded his eyes. After several years of wandering, he found Rapunzel and their twins in the wilderness. She gently healed his eyes with her tears. I want you to heal others' broken hearts as you comfort and mourn with them.

Proverbs 17:17, Romans 12:15

"Rapunzel" by Paul Hey

Snow White was "the fairest of them all," but was not vain. She was sweet and had a loving friendship with seven dwarfs who took her in and protected her from her evil stepmother, the Queen, who was jealous of her beauty and wanted her dead. I want you to recognize that inner beauty is far more important than outer beauty by always being loving, kind, helpful, and humble.

Galatians 5:22-23, 26

"The dwarfs leave Snow White in charge" by Franz Jüttner

Thumbelina might have been very small in size, but she had a big heart. After being kidnapped twice, she found refuge and friendship with a field mouse. Her new surroundings led her to an injured swallow, who she befriended and patiently and compassionately nursed back to health. I want you to always look around to see who needs assistance and then be a loving helper anytime you can.

Matthew 25:40, Galatians 6:2

"Thumbelina and the Swallow" by Arlena Lazareva

The Little Mermaid had a good heart with a desire for a human soul. She bravely rescued a drowning prince and fell in love with him. She made a dangerous bargain with a sea witch to become human, trading her voice for legs, in hopes that the prince would love her and marry her. Sadly, he fell in love with and married someone else. Brokenhearted, with her life at stake, she still chose to protect his life over her own. I want you to be brave and love selflessly like the Little Mermaid did.

St. John 15:13

"The Mermaid - in the sea" by Edmund Dulac

Each of these fairy-tale princesses were beautiful inside and out, and stayed that way, even though they endured difficult trials and heartaches. You can learn from them all.

You can also learn from each princess's mistakes and flaws.

Briar Rose used a spinning wheel without permission and without knowing how to use it, which led her to prick her finger.

"Briar Rose" by Anne Anderson

"Cinderella" by Valentine Cameron Prinsep

Cinderella was too afraid to tell her father how her stepmother and stepsisters treated her, and too afraid to tell the prince who she really was.

"Beauty broke an important promise to return to the Beast, almost causing his death.

"Beauty and the Beast" by Warwick Goble

"Rapunzel" by Paul Hey

Rapunzel needed to learn to stand up for herself and decide her own future. She didn't have to obey someone who only wanted to hurt her.

Snow White disobeyed the dwarfs more than once by trusting strangers who wanted to hurt her.

"The Queen visits Snow White" by Franz Jüttner

Thumbelina left her friends, the field mouse and the mole, without saying goodbye.

"'I know what you want' said the sea witch" by Harry Clarke

The Little Mermaid made an agreement with a sea witch to become human without considering the consequences if she couldn't keep her end of the deal.

Each of these princess's mistakes led to sadness and suffering, either for them or for those who loved them.

You can learn from these princesses to be careful, be truthful, keep your promises, listen to wise counsel, be courteous, and be brave. Also remember that it is your choice how you react to your trials. They are there for you to learn from and to help you be the best version of yourself that you can be.

Each of these fairy-tale princesses also had happy endings.

Briar Rose, the Sleeping Beauty, was awakened by the kiss of a courageous prince, whom she then married.

"Sleeping Beauty" by Henry Meynell Rheam

Cinderella married her prince after she was the only one who could fit into the gold shoe left at the ball.

"Finding that the slipper fits" by Hans Printz

Beauty broke the Beast's curse with her love, and they were married.

"Beauty and the Beast" by John Batten

After Rapunzel healed her husband's eyes with her tears, the prince led his wife and twins to his kingdom where they lived happily ever after.

Snow White came back to life when the poisoned apple dislodged from her throat and then married a prince who would protect her from her evil stepmother one last time.

"The Prince Awakes Snow White" by Franz Jüttner

Thumbelina married the prince of the flower people. She received the gift of wings and a new name: Maia.

The Little Mermaid, after refusing to hurt the prince to save her own life, became a daughter of the air with the ability to gain a soul someday.

In most of these fairy tales, the young woman is not a princess until she marries a prince.

I want you to know that you don't have to marry a prince or change anything about yourself to be a princess. Remember that you are already a princess, and always have been, because you are the daughter of a Heavenly King, your Heavenly Father.

He watches over you and sends angels, earthly and heavenly, to help you in your life. He also inspires you to be an angel to others.

To help you be an angel on earth, your Heavenly Father has lovingly given you special spiritual gifts you can use through your unique body.

Through your mind, you can gain knowledge, solve problems, and come up with great ideas.

Through your eyes, you can discern who is lonely, sad, or in need, learn from good books, and see beauty in the world.

Through your ears, you can be a good listener and hear words of wisdom.

Through your hands and arms, you can work hard, help and give to others, and hug or hold the hand of someone you love.

Through your voice, you can pray, tell the truth, invite, encourage, teach, inspire, compliment others, stand for what's right, and apologize when you make mistakes.

Through your feet, you can walk side by side with others and go wherever you are needed.

Through your heart, you can feel love, show kindness and compassion, treat others with tenderness, and see good in others, even those who are different or who aren't kind to you.

With your whole mind, body, and soul you can develop skills and talents that you can share with others.

Nurturing and sharing these gifts will help you be a wonderful friend, for everyone around you will feel that they belong and that they have worth. They will be able to feel Heavenly Father's love for them, just as you feel His love for you.

I hope you know that God's love is with you all the time, no matter how you are feeling or what you are going through. Sometimes you may not feel it, or think you deserve it, but it's always there.

And always remember it's okay to be different. Your Heavenly Father created you exactly the way you are supposed to be.

I want you to always remember who you are and to truly believe that you are a spiritual young lady who has unlimited divine potential.

I know you have a divine mission to fulfill on this earth that you are already fulfilling. Embrace it and know that your earthly and Heavenly parents will be with you through it all.

I love you always, my Princess.

Dedicated to all the moms who love their princesses.

Imprint: Independently published

Pictures from Pixabay, Istock, Dreamstime, Wikipedia, AdobeStock, Pexels, and personal photos.

Made in the USA
Monee, IL
02 July 2025

20395135R00024